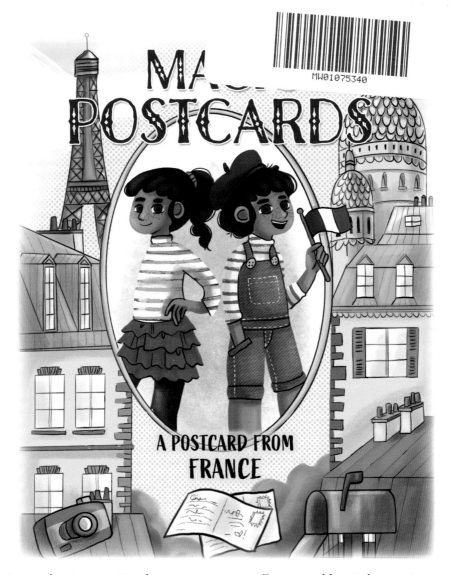

MAGIC POSTCARDS

A POSTCARD FROM FRANCE

Written by Laurie Friedman   Illustrated by Roberta Ravasio

A Blossoms Beginning Readers Book

CRABTREE
Publishing Company
www.crabtreebooks.com

Level 1 Early Emergent Readers Grades PK-K

Books at this level have strong picture support with carefully controlled text and repetitive patterns. They feature a limited number of words on each page and large, easy-to-read print.

Level 2 Emergent Readers Grade 1

Books at this level have a more complex sentence structure and more lines of text per page. They depend less on repetitive patterns and pictures. Familiar topics are explored, but with greater depth.

Level 3 Early Readers Grade 2

Books at this level are carefully developed to tell a great story, but in a format that children are able to read and enjoy by themselves. They feature familiar vocabulary and appealing illustrations.

Level 4 Fluent Readers Grade 3

Books at this level have more text and use challenging vocabulary. They explore less familiar topics and continue to help refine and strengthen reading skills to get ready for chapter books.

School-to-Home Support for Caregivers and Teachers

This book helps children grow by letting them practice reading. Here are a few guiding questions to help the reader with building his or her comprehension skills. Possible answers appear here in red.

Before Reading:

• What do I think this story will be about?
  • *I think this story will be about the monuments and museums in France.*
  • *I think this story will be about the different cities in France.*

During Reading:

• Pause and look at the words and pictures. Why did the character do that?
  • *I think the twins and Pierre stopped at the River Seine because Pierre wanted to explain about the thirty-seven bridges that connect the Left Bank to the Right Bank.*
  • *I think Pierre took the twins to the Louvre because it's the biggest museum in the world.*

After Reading:

• Describe your favorite part of the story.
  • *My favorite part was when they were riding bikes through the French countryside.*
  • *I liked seeing the kids riding past a lavender field on their bikes—it was so pretty.*

Camila and Carlos stood in front of their mailbox.

"Your turn," said Carlos.

Slowly, Camila opened the mailbox.

Another postcard!

She read it out loud to her brother.

Dear Camila and Carlos,
Hold this card.
Close your eyes.
Count to ten.
Wait for a surprise.
See you soon!

Pierre

"Where are we going?" asked Carlos.

Camila turned the postcard over.

A map of France was on the back.

Camila and Carlos were going to France!

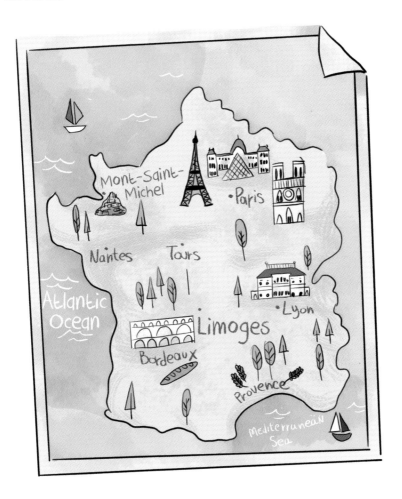

"Ready?" asked Camila.

Carlos nodded. Camila and Carlos held the postcard.

They closed their eyes and counted.

One
Two
Three
Four
Five
Six
Seven
Eight
Nine
Ten

Camila and Carlos opened their eyes.
They were at a small cafe.
A boy greeted them.
He told them his name was Pierre.
"Welcome to France!" said Pierre.

Carlos and Camila ate breakfast.
Pierre told them about the day ahead.
"We start our tour in Paris," he said.
"Then we see the French countryside."

"Your postcard will take us from place to place," said Pierre.

Camila tucked the postcard into her pocket.

"Let's begin!" said Pierre.

Camila and Carlos followed Pierre down a cobblestone street.

"Paris is the capital of France," said Pierre.

"It is a very old and beautiful city."

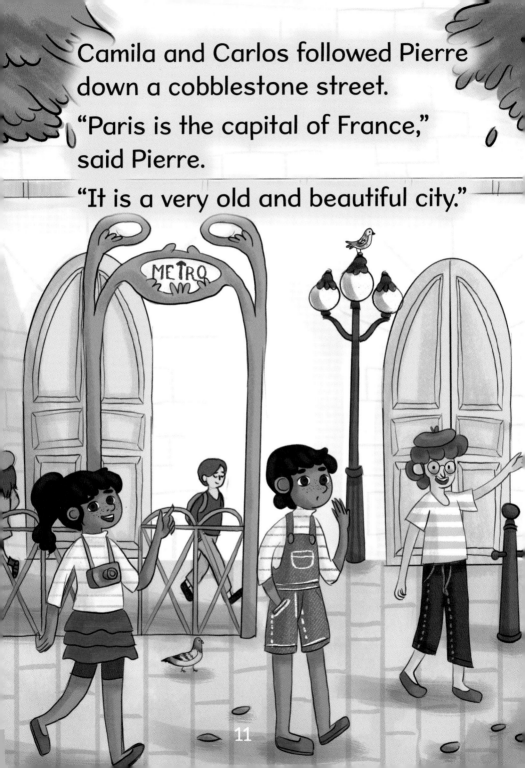

Camila, Carlos, and Pierre walked the streets of Paris.

They saw fancy buildings. Tall churches. Famous monuments.

Camila took lots of pictures.

Hôtel de Ville

Arc de Triomphe

Notre-Dame

They stopped on a bridge.

"The River Seine splits the city of Paris in half," explained Pierre.

"Thirty-seven bridges connect the Left Bank to the Right Bank."

"That's a lot of bridges!" said Carlos.

Camila's tummy rumbled.

"Time for lunch!"
said Pierre.

They stood in line to
buy crepes.

PARIS CREPES

€5,00
PLUS
CHOCO

Then they went to a park to eat them.

Carlos liked the crepe filled with cheese.

Camila liked the crepe filled with chocolate!

After lunch, Pierre took Carlos and Camila to a museum.

"This is the Louvre," said Pierre.

"It's huge!" said Camila.

Pierre smiled. "It's the biggest museum in the world."

Carlos and Camila only had time to see a few of the paintings inside.

The Mo

"Next up, the Eiffel Tower," said Pierre. "No trip to Paris is complete until you've seen it."

18

Carlos put his head back so he could see all the way to the top.

"Ready to go up?" asked Pierre.

Carlos and Camila followed Pierre inside.

Up and up they went . . . until they got to the top!

"WOW!" said Carlos when he saw the view.

"Paris is so pretty!" said Camila.

"It is a special city," said Pierre.

It was time to visit some other special places in France.

Camila and Carlos held their postcard and closed their eyes.

When they opened them, they were on a small island.

"We're at Mont-Saint-Michel," said Pierre. "It's in the north of France."

Pierre took them on a tour of the ancient walled city.

Pierre, Camila, and Carlos walked the narrow streets.

They climbed steep stairs to the top. Then they took a picture together.

"I'll never forget this day," said Camila.

Pierre smiled. "It's not over yet!"

Camila and Carlos held their postcard and blinked.

Mont-Saint-Michel

Suddenly, they were in a rowboat.

"Now we're in central France," said Pierre. He pointed to a fancy country house.

"That is a chateau. Many years ago, kings, queens, and nobility built these homes.

They would stay in them to get away from city life."

Carlos posed with the magic postcard. Camila took his picture. Then it was time to head south.

Chateau du Chambord

Carlos and Camila held their postcard and closed their eyes.

When they opened them, they were surrounded by rocky cliffs.

"Do you like to ride bikes?" asked Pierre.

"We love it!" Carlos and Camila said at the same time.

"We are in Provence," said Pierre.

"We will ride bikes so you can see the French countryside."

Pierre, Camila, and Carlos rode and rode.

They passed fruit orchards. And fields of flowers.

They stopped at a market to shop.

Camila bought cheese.

Carlos bought a long, thin loaf of
bread called a baguette.

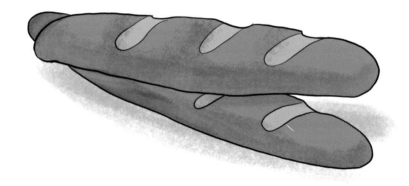

The Sun was starting to set.

It was time to return home.

"Thank you for showing us your country," said Camila and Carlos.

"I hope you will come back one day," said Pierre.

Camila and Carlos promised to return.

Then they held their postcard and closed their eyes.

Camila and Carlos were back home.
With happy memories of their special
day in France.

ABOUT THE AUTHOR

Laurie Friedman is the award-winning author of more than seventy-five critically acclaimed picture books, chapter books, and novels for young readers, including the bestselling *Mallory McDonald* series and the *Love, Ruby Valentine* series. She is a native Arkansan, and in addition to writing, loves to read, bake, do yoga, and spend time with her friends and family. For more information about Laurie and her books, please visit her website at www.lauriebfriedman.com.

ABOUT THE ILLUSTRATOR

Roberta Ravasio was born in a farmhouse in Bergamo, Italy. She attended the high school of arts in her city and later moved to Milan, where she completed the School of Comics. In her work she uses a combination of traditional and digital media, and creates characters, greeting cards, books, and more. When she is not drawing, she loves playing with her son, running, and watching TV dramas.

CRABTREE
Publishing Company

Written by: Laurie Friedman

Illustrations by: Roberta Ravasio

Art direction and layout by: Rhea Wallace

Series Development: James Earley

Proofreader: Melissa Boyce

Educational Consultant: Marie Lemke M.Ed.

Library and Archives Canada
Cataloguing in Publication

CIP available at Library and Archives
Canada

Library of Congress Cataloging-in-
Publication Data

CIP available at Library of Congress

Crabtree Publishing Company

www.crabtreebooks.com   1-800-387-7650

Printed in the U.S.A./CG20210915/012022

Published in the United States
Crabtree Publishing
347 Fifth Avenue, Suite 1402-145
New York, NY, 10016

Published in Canada
Crabtree Publishing
616 Welland Ave.
St. Catharines, ON, L2M 5V6